ABOUT THE BANK STREET READY-TO-READ SERIES

More than seventy-five years of educational research, innovative teaching, and quality publishing have earned The Bank Street College of Education its reputation as America's most trusted name in early childhood education.

Because no two children are exactly alike in their development, the Bank Street Ready-to-Read series is written on three levels to accommodate the individual stages of reading readiness of children ages three through eight.

- *Level 1:* **GETTING READY TO READ (Pre-K–Grade 1)**
  Level 1 books are perfect for reading aloud with children who are getting ready to read or just starting to read words or phrases. These books feature large type, repetition, and simple sentences.

- *Level 2:* **READING TOGETHER (Grades 1–3)**
  These books have slightly smaller type and longer sentences. They are ideal for children beginning to read by themselves who may need help.

- *Level 3:* **I CAN READ IT MYSELF (Grades 2–3)**
  These stories are just right for children who can read independently. They offer more complex and challenging stories and sentences.

All three levels of The Bank Street Ready-to-Read books make it easy to select the books most appropriate for your child's development and enable him or her to grow with the series step by step. The levels purposely overlap to reinforce skills and further encourage reading.

We feel that making reading fun is the single most important thing anyone can do to help children become good readers. We hope you will become part of Bank Street's long tradition of learning through sharing.

The Bank Street College of Education

To Fred, who shared the experience
— B.B.

To the Dickermans
— E.A.M.

For a free color catalog describing Gareth Stevens' list of high-quality books and multimedia programs, call 1-800-542-2595 (USA) or 1-800-461-9120 (Canada). Gareth Stevens Publishing's Fax: (414) 225-0377. See our catalog, too, on the World Wide Web: http://gsinc.com

Library of Congress Cataloging-in-Publication Data

Brenner, Barbara.
    Beavers beware! / by Barbara Brenner; illustrated by Emily Arnold McCully.
        p. cm. -- (Bank Street ready-to-read)
    Summary: A family with a house on the river finds two beavers cutting down trees and building a lodge on their dock.
    ISBN 0-8368-1769-9 (lib. bdg.)
    1. Beavers--Juvenile fiction. [1. Beavers--Fiction.] I. McCully, Emily Arnold, ill.
II. Title. III. Series.
PZ10.3.B753Be   1998
[E]--dc21   97-47621

This edition first published in 1998 by
Gareth Stevens Publishing
1555 North RiverCenter Drive, Suite 201
Milwaukee, Wisconsin 53212 USA

© 1992 by Byron Preiss Visual Publications, Inc. Text © 1992 by Bank Street College of Education. Illustrations © 1992 by Emily Arnold McCully and Byron Preiss Visual Publications, Inc.

Published by arrangement with Bantam Doubleday Dell Books For Young Readers, a division of Bantam Doubleday Dell Publishing Group, Inc., New York, New York. All rights reserved.

Bank Street Ready To Read™ is a registered U.S. trademark of the Bank Street Group and Bantam Doubleday Dell Books For Young Readers, a division of Bantam Doubleday Dell Publishing Group, Inc.

Printed in Mexico

1 2 3 4 5 6 7 8 9 02 01 00 99 98

Bank Street Ready-to-Read™

BEAVERS BEWARE!

by Barbara Brenner
Illustrated by Emily Arnold McCully

A Byron Preiss Book

Gareth Stevens Publishing
MILWAUKEE

E
BRE

This is our house
by the river.
This is our dock,
where the story begins.

One day we find
two little sticks lying
on the dock.
We know right away
they are not any old sticks.
They are too clean and slick.

The next day three more sticks
show up.
They're clean and slick, too.

I say, "What happened to the bark on these sticks?"
Dad says,
"Maybe an animal ate it."
We throw the sticks away.

The next day there are
more sticks on the dock,
and a big branch, too.
We take the sticks away.
We drag the branch away.

Pretty soon there are
ten sticks, two branches,
and a big tree on the dock.
They are each cut to a point.

"What animal could do this?"
I ask.
"An animal with sharp teeth,"
my dad says.

9

Every day we take away
sticks, branches, and trees.
But the next day new ones
always show up.

10

"I'd like to see that animal," I say.
Mom says, "It must come
at night."

Then one day I am
swimming off the dock.
WHOOSH!
Two heads pop up
out of the water.
I get a quick look at
brown fur and round heads.
I see a flash of orange teeth.
SMACK!
A tail slaps the water.
They dive and are gone.
I know what they are.
BEAVERS!

I tell Mom and Dad.
"There are two beavers
at the dock!"
"Beavers eat bark," Dad says.
Mom says, "And they build
with sticks and branches.
They must be building a lodge."

By the next week the lodge
is taller than my dad.
Mom says,
"If you put beavers by water,
they'll start building.
And once they get going,
they won't stop."

The week after that
the beavers stuff the cracks
in the lodge with clam shells
and old rags and string.
It begins to look like a junk pile.

The week after that
they begin to build under the dock.
Mom dives down to take a look.

"There's a tunnel down here,"
she calls.
"It leads up to that space
under the dock.
It's dry there.
That must be where they sleep."
"Pretty clever," I say.
"Pretty messy," says Dad.

The next week the beavers
put mud all over their lodge.
They put their own smell
on the mud
to keep other beavers away.
Dad says, "That smell would keep
anybody away."

Now the beavers begin
to cut down big trees.
Mom gets mad about the trees.
"Animals have rights," I say.
"Trees have rights, too," she says.

The beavers move in.
By day they sleep under our dock.
At dusk they eat the water plants.
At night they cut down our trees.

"This is war," my dad says.
"I'm calling the game warden.
He can trap the beavers alive
and move them."

"What about animal rights?" I ask.
"What about people rights?"
Mom asks.

But that night
there is a storm.
The wind howls.

There are big waves
on the river.
Sometime that night
the dock floats loose.

In the morning
everything is gone—
dock, sticks, mud,
trees, junk, smell—
and the beavers!
I say to Dad,
"If this is war,
the beavers win!"

I still think about those beavers.
I think of them
floating down the river
on our dock.
Or maybe they're chewing away
with those big orange teeth,
building a new lodge.

We're building, too.
We're building a new dock.
Only this time—
no beavers allowed.

and my elephant reads to them.